The God of Grandma Forever

The God of Grandma Forever

Margriet Hogeweg

Translated by Nancy Forest-Flier

Front Street

Asheville, North Carolina

First edition

Library of Congress Cataloging-in-Publication Data
Hogeweg, Margriet.
[God van oma Vanouds. English]
The God of Grandma Forever / Margriet Hogeweg;
translated by Nancy Forest-Flier.
p. cm.
Summary: When her Grandma Forever comes to
live in her attic, Maria must discover how to deal with her
difficult behavior and talk of God.
ISBN 1-886910-69-3 (alk. paper)
[1. Grandmothers-Fiction. 2. God-Fiction.]
I. Forest, Nancy. II. Title.
PZ7.H6835 Go 2001
[Fic]-dc21   00-051073

For Barend

When He came in, He said to them,
"Why make this commotion and weep?
The child is not dead, but sleeping."
And they ridiculed Him.

Mark 5:39-40a

The God of Grandma Forever

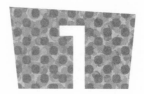

Maria had two grandmas. They weren't anything like the grandmas of the other children in her class or in her neighborhood, not by a long shot. When Maria went to visit them, they never gave her candy or cookies. And when she got a good report card, the grandmas kept their wallets shut tight. One of the grandmas wouldn't even let Maria in when she came knocking. And the other swore at Maria when she was angry. But Maria didn't care. Because even though the grandmas didn't act like most grandmas do, they were very special just the same.

One of the two grandmas lived in Maria's house, upstairs in the attic. She had a little bronze bell that she rang whenever she wanted something. This grandma had the same first name as Maria, and the same last name, too – Van Dalen. But because she was so terribly old (she was ninety-three), Maria called her Grandma Forever. It seemed to suit her better.

Although Maria liked the idea of having a grandma come to live in her house, she was dead set against her coming to live in the attic because it really was Maria's attic. That's where she played hide-and-seek with her friend Jacob, between the old boxes of yellowed books and dusty chests filled with mysterious junk. Or sometimes they dressed up as pirates. Maria and Jacob tied black patches over one eye and red kerchiefs around their heads. The attic was their ship, and they hung out of the dormer window with a pair of binoculars in search of any other pirates who might be lurking around. For hours on end they gazed out over the sea of rooftops, and when they finally spied land they lit a rocket that Jacob had leftover from New Year's. Their parents would never have let them do anything like that, of course, but they made sure nobody saw them.

Maria also went to the attic when she was sad. If she had to cry, she rocked herself to sleep in the hammock that hung between the beams. Maria called it her comfort hammock, because when she woke up after sleeping in it she usually had forgotten why she had cried so hard. She was always surprised to discover that the sleep had dried up her sadness like a warm radiator.

The attic was also a good place for thinking about things, especially at the end of the afternoon, when the sun shone through the window and the blackbird on the rooftop sang so beautifully that it gave Maria goose bumps. That was the best time to get started with the big cleanup in her head.

Every now and then Maria had to straighten up her mind, the same way she had to straighten up her bedroom. If she didn't, everything would get lost, and she wouldn't be able to find anything at all. One time she waited too long to do her cleanup, and everything was in such a mess in her mind that she kept on stumbling over all the piles of ideas and memories lying around. She didn't want that to happen again.

Whenever Maria thought it was time for another big cleanup in her head, she would hop into the creaky rocking chair that stood in the middle of all the junk in the attic. Then she would start rocking until everything was back in place. She put all the good ideas in a neat little pile at the front of her head so she could see them easily. On top of the pile was the idea of building a tree house in the cemetery. She thought it would be so exciting – she and Jacob spying on people who came to visit the graves. But Jacob was afraid to go to the cemetery. He was afraid of the people who were lying there, and she hadn't found anybody else to build a tree house with who was as much fun as Jacob.

The bad ideas disappeared into the wastebasket where everything went that Maria didn't need anymore or that she wanted to forget. Just the other day she had thrown away the idea of switching parents with Jacob. At first Jacob's father and mother seemed much nicer than her own father and mother, because Jacob was allowed to stay up later and because he had more toys. But then Jacob told her that his father had given him a spanking, just because he had climbed out onto the roof of his house to try to see Maria in her pirate ship. That wasn't the kind of father Maria wanted to have.

If there were things in her head that Maria didn't understand very well, she looked at them this way and that. Sometimes that helped. Maria had a little pile for things that she did understand. That's where she had just put the answer her mother had given her when she asked why she was an only child: "Because you're my one and only." That means I'm special, Maria thought. Special kids are nice. And I am nice, I guess. So I understand that.

Maria also had a pile for some things she just couldn't understand, no matter how much she wanted to or how hard she tried. Yesterday her mother had said something to her that she didn't get at all. She and Jacob had tried to jump over the brook, and she had missed. She came home soaking wet with green weeds in her hair.

"You look like you're part boy," said her mother, as Maria stood there dripping on the kitchen mat. When she went to put on dry clothes, Maria studied herself in the mirror. What she saw was all girl, not part boy. Boys had penises. She didn't. Not even part of one. She didn't know what she should do with what her mother had said, throw it away or save it awhile? She decided to save it, just to be on the safe side. You never know.

She also had all sorts of memories rattling around in her head. Maria gathered up all the nice memories, and all the funny ones, and looked at them one by one. But she swept the unpleasant memories into a dark corner of her mind as fast as she could, to a place she didn't visit very often. That's where she had put the memory of the little kitten she had played with one day outside. Without warning the kitten had darted into the street, and a car had run over it. It lay there on the cobblestones deathly still. Blood trickled from its mouth. Maria couldn't watch. She ran away. Crying, she crept into her hammock in the attic. But this time when she woke the sadness hadn't dried up. The next day the kitten was gone, but in her mind she still could see it lying there. She had tried to throw the bad memory of the accident far, far away, but it seemed to have legs of its own. It would pop up at the most unexpected moments and run through her head like a disobedient dog.

By the time the sun had gone down and the first stars had appeared it was usually as peaceful in Maria's head as it was outside. The blackbird had found a place to sleep by then. Hidden deep among the leaves of a tall tree, he would nod off slowly, with his head tucked under his feathers. Then Maria would jump out of her rocking chair and leave the attic with her head all straightened up and tidy.

One day Maria's father and mother told her that grandma was coming to live in the attic. Maria became very, very angry. Where was she supposed to go if she had to do some deep thinking or hard crying? And where could she and Jacob play hide-and-seek or pirate? But no matter what she said, her parents thought it was nonsense.

"You can play with Jacob in your own room," they said, "or outside." As if that was the same thing, Maria thought.

"And you can think and cry anywhere you want," they said. Maria had never heard anything so silly in her life. Her idea was to stick grandma in the little room under the stairs where the vacuum cleaner and the ironing board were now. They could easily get grandma's bed in there with a little pushing and shoving. All grandma did was lie around in bed all day anyway, so she didn't need much room, Maria thought. But her father and mother said that wouldn't do.

"We don't stick you in a closet under the stairs," said her father.

"No, but I don't lie around in bed all day."

"Grandma's not going to do that either," her father said.

"Want to bet?"

It turned out that Maria was right. Grandma only came out from under the covers to pee in the potty that she kept under her bed. The rest of the day she did nothing but lie there.

Early in the morning, when her potty was filled to the brim, grandma would ring her bronze bell. Then the potty had to be carried downstairs and emptied in the toilet. Sometimes that was Maria's job. Maria thought it was really disgusting, because grandma's pee smelled to high heaven. Even so, her mother never let her hold her nose when she carried grandma's potty down the stairs. But a few days ago the smell had made her so sick that she held her nose anyway and the potty slipped out of her hands. Everything was covered with grandma's pee. She and her mother spent a whole hour cleaning the stairs. They used every kind of detergent in the kitchen cupboard, but it didn't help. When you stood on the stairwell it still smelled like grandma's pee.

"It's enough to make a tomcat jealous," Maria's mother said.

"It's your own fault," said Maria. "You shouldn't have given my attic away to grandma."

Grandma Forever wasn't Maria's only grandma. She had another, but that one didn't live in the attic. The other grandma slept under a big stone in the cemetery at the end of the street, and her name was Grandma Bedstone. Her name was so beautiful, Maria thought, that she didn't need to think up a new one for her.

Maria liked to visit Grandma Bedstone. Every Wednesday afternoon she would crawl through a hole in the hedge that grew around the cemetery like a green fence. Grandma Bedstone lay buried under a stone that was as white as a peppermint. Her name was written on the stone in licorice-black letters. Whenever she came to visit, Maria knocked on the stone three times with her fist.

"Hello, Grandma Bedstone. It's me, Maria," she would say.

Grandma Bedstone never opened the door, no matter how hard Maria knocked. Maria could talk to her, though, and if she listened carefully she could hear her grandma's voice. If Grandma Bedstone was in a good mood she would tell Maria stories about the worms and the bugs that lived right underneath the stone or about the darkest dark on earth where she was lying. Everything grandma told her was beautiful, Maria thought. But her mother didn't think so. Whenever she tried to talk about grandma's stories her mother would get angry.

"Where do you get it from, all this gruesome nonsense?"

"From grandma."

Maria's mother didn't believe a word of it – that Grandma Bedstone told stories or that grandma's bed lay under the stone.

"Grandma is dead," she said. "The only thing under that stone are grandma's bones, and if you hear something in your head it's your own imagination. Why don't you go to the playground and play with your girlfriends? A cemetery is no place for children."

When Maria's mother said things like that, Maria would shrug her shoulders as if she didn't care at all.

"How many children do you have?" Maria asked Grandma Forever. She had just brought grandma's meal upstairs on a wooden tray and was now sitting on a stool beside grandma's bed.

"Eleven," said grandma as she stuck a forkful of brown rice into her mouth.

Maria looked at grandma's belly in astonishment.

"Were they all in your belly?"

"They sure were. Not all eleven at once, of course."

"No. I know that," said Maria impatiently. "You could have twins. Or triplets. But elevenlets is kind of a lot."

She watched as grandma slowly cleaned her plate. Every day she got the same thing: brown rice with carrots, a raw vegetable salad, and cottage cheese with oranges for dessert. One time, when Maria was halfway up the stairs, she had taken a taste of grandma's brown rice. It was awful, she thought. The little skins on the grains of rice tickled her tongue and stuck to the roof of her mouth. She didn't understand how grandma could like it. Grandma also drank bright orange carrot juice and purple beet juice. But Maria never dared take a sip because it looked like poison.

Maria's mother once explained to her why grandma only ate and drank those strange things.

"Grandma thinks she has cancer. That's why she's on the Moerman Diet. She thinks the special food will make her better."

"Is that why grandma lies around in bed all day?"

"Yes, and because she's so old."

"Does grandma really have cancer?" asked Maria.

"No, grandma doesn't have cancer. She just thinks she does."

"Why does she think she does?"

"Because grandpa died of cancer."

"Is cancer catching?"

"No, smarty-pants."

"So why does grandma think she has it?"

"I couldn't tell you, honey. Your grandma isn't completely normal."

Maria had never seen Grandpa Forever. He slept under a stone, just like Grandma Bedstone, but in a much bigger cemetery at the other end of town. She went there with her father once. Too bad it was so far away, Maria thought, otherwise she would visit her grandpa every week, too.

"You're daddy's mother, right?" Maria asked Grandma Forever.

"That's right. I'm your father's mother."

"So daddy was in your belly, too?"

"I'll say," said grandma. "But your father was a big nuisance. He didn't want to come out. He was born by cesarean section."

"What's that?"

"If a baby doesn't want to come out, the doctor makes a hole in your belly and takes him out that way. Then the doctor sews the hole closed and there's nothing left but a scar."

"Can I see it?"

Grandma put the tray with the empty plate on the nightstand next to her bed. She threw the blankets off and pulled up her pink nightgown and then her white undershirt. Across her naked belly was a long scar. Pirates had scars like that, Maria thought, but they had them on their faces.

"Wow," said Maria. "I want a scar like that some-day, too. Then I'll be as tough as Captain Hook."

"Who is Captain Hook, for heaven's sake?" asked grandma.

"He's a pirate."

"Pirates don't exist anymore," said grandma.

"They do, too, dummy," said Maria angrily.

"Smart aleck," said grandma, pulling down her undershirt and nightgown. She smoothed out the blankets with her long fingers. "The Lord will punish you. Now get out of my attic. I have to listen to the minister."

"It's not your attic. You can borrow it, but it's still my attic."

Grandma waved her away with her skinny hand and turned the radio up full blast.

"Grandma Forever said the Lord is going to punish me," said Maria, scooping a big potato onto her plate.

"Jonathan, I don't want your mother talking that nonsense to Maria," said Maria's mother. She served herself some spinach and hurled the serving spoon back into the pan. Maria could see her mother was angry. She usually didn't throw spoons around, and she called daddy Jonathan only when she was angry about something. Otherwise she just called him Jon.

"Oh, you know how my mother is," said Maria's father. "She doesn't mean any harm."

"Even so, I don't want her saying such things," said her mother.

"She must have had her reasons, you can be sure of that," said her father.

"All I did was call grandma dummy."

"That was a very fresh thing to say," said her father sternly, but Maria saw the twinkle in his eyes.

"Who is the Lord anyway?" asked Maria.

"The Lord is the same as God," said Maria's father.

"Do you listen to the word of God?" Maria asked.

"Here we go again!" said Maria's mother.

Maria stopped eating. "What do you mean?" she asked.

Her mother didn't say anything. She shoved her chair backwards and grabbed a jar of applesauce from the counter.

"Mom, did you know you can hear the word of God on the radio every Sunday?"

"You must have heard that from grandma," her mother muttered.

Maria nodded, her mouth full of food.

"Don't believe everything grandma tells you."

The word of God wasn't the only thing grandma listened to on the radio. She also listened to the minister, the orchestra, and the man who did the news. Maria really wanted to hear the word of God, but grandma wouldn't let her. "You can't sit still," she had once said when Maria asked if she could stay to listen.

"How does grandma know that the Lord is going to punish me? Did she hear it on the radio?" asked Maria.

"On the radio? Whatever gave you that idea? Grandma cooked that up all by herself," said her mother, and she still sounded angry.

"Like the cancer?"

"Yes, sort of. Now finish your supper."

Maria mashed her potatoes hard and made a little well in the middle for the gravy. The potatoes were the mountains, the gravy was the lake, and the spinach was the forest. She imagined that the food on her plate was the Land of Mush. Maria stuck her knife and fork into the mountains and gave the Land of Mush a good stirring. This is an earthquake, she thought.

As soon as her plate was empty, grandma's bell started to ring.

"I'll go," said Maria. Slowly she walked upstairs. She could have gone faster, but she knew that running was bad if you'd just eaten. At least that's what her mother always said.

"Is that you again, smart aleck?" said grandma as Maria entered her bedroom.

Maria nodded.

"Ask your mother if she's remembered that the minister is coming by tonight."

Maria was back on the top step when grandma called after her, "And don't let her serve those cheap cookies with the coffee. Ministers should have a nice thick slice of cake, not some dried-up old cookie."

"What did grandma want?" Maria's mother asked when she got back to the kitchen.

"She said the minister was coming by tonight and that he wants cake with his coffee, not a cookie."

Her mother let out a deep sigh.

A broad grin spread across her father's face.

"I don't see what's so funny, Jonathan," said Maria's mother. "I'm glad I'm not going to be here tonight. You figure out what to do with that mother of yours."

"Are we going to bake a cake?" Maria asked her father.

"Not on your life. The minister will take potluck with his coffee," said her mother.

"And what's in the pot?" asked Maria.

"There are still a few cupcakes in the drawer under the stove," Maria's mother said from the doorway. "I'm going upstairs to get dressed. Will you two do the dishes tonight?"

Maria's father shut the kitchen door softly. He drew his index finger up to his mouth.

"How about doing the dishes Finnish style, after the news and *The Simpsons*?" he whispered slyly.

"Great," Maria whispered back. "Finnish style."

When Maria's mother wasn't home, Maria and her

father always did the dishes Finnish style. They left everything in the rack to drain by itself – dishes, cups, glasses, and silverware. They didn't dry anything. Maria's father had told her that that's how people in Finland did the dishes and that they even had special cabinets where you could put plates and cups to drain.

Maria's mother didn't like Finnish-style dishwashing. She thought it made the dishes smell bad. Sometimes Maria's mother went away on vacation alone for a week. When she came home, she would sniff the plates and glasses like a little dog.

"Ugh, you didn't dry the dishes again, did you?" she'd yell. "They smell awful."

Maria's mother peeked around the corner of the living room door. Her lips were as red as strawberries, and her eyes were black around the edges. Long glittering earrings hung from her ears. She always looked like that when she was going out for the evening.

"Have fun," said her father.

"You too, with the minister," said Maria's mother.

"The minister's coming for grandma, not for us," said her father.

"Don't forget to do the dishes."

"We'll get to those later," said Maria's father.

Maria ran to her mother and gave her a kiss on her red mouth. Now she had a red mouth too. "No, no," she said when her mother tried to wipe the kiss away. Then her mother blew a kiss to her father. Her father caught it and stuffed it into the pocket of his pants.

"Where are you going?" Maria asked her mother.

"To the movies with Aunt Margie. Be a good girl for daddy, okay?"

A car horn tooted outside. "That's her," said her mother. "Bye-bye." She closed the living room door behind her. Maria heard her mother's heels clicking in the hallway. The front door locked shut with a bang.

"So, now we have the kingdom to ourselves," said Maria's father. He grabbed his newspaper and started to read.

"Shall we play a game?" asked Maria.

"Not now. I'm reading the paper."

Maria began to watch television without really seeing anything. She just hoped the minister would come before she had to go to bed.

"Is the minister who's coming tonight the minister on grandma's radio?"

"No, the minister coming tonight is another minister. He's the minister from the church. Be quiet now. I'm reading the paper."

Maria knew where the church was. She passed it on the way to school.

The doorbell rang.

"There he is," shouted Maria. "Can I let him in?"

There at the door stood a well-dressed gentleman. He looked like a crow. Everything about him was black: his coat, the suit under his coat, the briefcase in one hand, and the umbrella in the other hand. Only his shirt and his face were white, as white as a sheet.

"Good evening, young lady," said the gentleman in black. He spoke very slowly and properly. "I am the minister."

"And I am Maria," said Maria.

The minister looked at the red kiss on Maria's lips.

"May I come in?" he asked.

"Fine with me," said Maria.

She stepped to the side, and the minister walked through the doorway. He took off his coat and hung it on a hook in the hall. The umbrella took its place on the hook next to his coat.

"I've come to see your grandma," he said.

"Grandma lives with us up in the attic," said Maria.

She pointed to the stairs at the end of the hallway.

"I know," said the minister, "but first I'd like to see your father and mother for a moment."

"My mother isn't here," said Maria. "She went to the movies."

"Ah, yes," said the minister. "But your father – he's here, isn't he?"

"Yes," said Maria. "But I don't know if he wants to talk to you because he's reading the paper. He never wants to talk when he's reading the paper."

"Please come in, Reverend," Maria heard her father say as he walked up from behind her. "I see you've already met my daughter."

The minister shook Maria's father's hand.

"Are you well?" asked the minister.

"Very well, thank you," said Maria's father. He was talking almost as properly as the minister. "Would you like a cup of coffee?"

"Please," said the minister.

"You know how to get to the attic, I assume?" asked her father.

"Yes, indeed," said the minister.

Maria and her father went into the kitchen to make coffee. The minister went up to the attic to see grandma. His shiny black leather shoes squeaked on the stairs.

Maria's father scooped the coffee out of the canister into a paper filter and put the filter into the coffeemaker. He then filled the coffeemaker with water and pushed the red button. Maria took the cupcakes out of the drawer under the stove and put two of them on a round dish.

"Can we have one, too?" asked Maria.

"Later," said her father. "First grandma and the minister."

The coffeemaker began gurgling. Little clouds of steam came out. When the weather was very cold and Maria went outside, the same kinds of little clouds came out of her mouth. Her father poured the coffee into two very fancy cups with saucers under them. They were visitor cups. Her father and mother always drank their coffee from ordinary mugs. Maria put the dish with the cupcakes on the tray next to the coffee cups, the little pitcher of milk, and the bowl of sugar.

"Be careful on the stairs with that tray," cautioned her father. "And knock politely before you go in. And don't say anything weird to the minister."

Maria carefully walked up the two sets of stairs to the attic. She wondered why it was so bad to say weird things to the minister. She put the tray on the floor in front of grandma's door. Behind the door she heard the hum of the minister's voice. Maria could tell it wasn't the same minister that grandma listened to on the radio. The radio minister didn't hum; he roared like a lion with an empty stomach. Maria knocked on the attic door quietly.

"Come in," said grandma.

Maria opened the door. Grandma and the minister watched as she lifted the tray with the coffee and cupcakes from the floor.

"I hope your mother vacuumed, or there'll be bits of dust floating in the coffee," said grandma. Maria looked at the coffee.

"I don't see anything," she said. "There's only coffee floating in the coffee."

Grandma scowled at her.

"Children are so fresh these days," she said to the minister.

The minister moved his head. Maria couldn't tell if he had nodded yes or shaken his head no. It was a little of both, she thought. She put the tray on grandma's nightstand.

"What's that mess you've smeared on your lips?" grandma asked Maria.

"It's not a mess. It's a lipstick kiss. I got it from mom." Grandma pulled down the corners of her mouth.

"Ugh," she said. "Now get lost, smart aleck. There's nothing here for you. Get out of my attic."

"My attic," corrected Maria.

Maria wished she could stay a minute to hear what grandma and the minister were talking about, but her grandma looked as if she meant business.

Maria shut the door behind her, but she didn't go downstairs right away. She stayed in the dark hall and pressed her ear to the door. At least now she could hear what Grandma Forever and the minister were saying to each other. The minister was talking about the weather.

"It's rather nice for this time of year," he said to grandma. "Do you ever go out for a walk?"

"Walk?" asked grandma. "Do you think my son has time for such things?"

"Your granddaughter perhaps?" asked the minister. Maria strained her ears. They were talking about her.

"With that smart aleck? I wouldn't dream of it," said grandma. "Do you know what she said to me today? She called me dummy!"

Suddenly someone put a hand over Maria's mouth and pulled her away from the door. Maria struggled to get free, but she was being carried down the stairs by two strong arms and then put down on the floor in front of her bedroom door. The light in the hall went on. The arms were those of her father. And so were the furiously glaring eyes.

"What's gotten into you?" her father asked. "Snooping around like that outside grandma's door. You know that's not allowed."

Maria looked at the toes of her shoes.

"Go to bed. I'm very angry with you," said her father.

Maria got undressed in her bedroom. She put on her pajamas and went to the bathroom. With a wet washcloth she wiped her mother's lipstick off her mouth. Then she brushed her teeth. She could hear her father downstairs doing the dishes by himself.

I didn't even get a cupcake, thought Maria as she climbed into bed with tears stinging her eyes. And now daddy's mad, too. He didn't even give me a goodnight kiss.

The door of grandma's attic room opened. Maria heard the minister's shoes squeaking back down the stairs. The visit with grandma was already over.

"I'll be going now," said the minister in the hallway downstairs.

The door of Maria's room was open a crack. She did

her best not to listen to what the minister said to her father. If her father knew she was eavesdropping again he'd be angrier than ever. But with the minister and her father talking so loudly, she couldn't help but hear.

"Thank you for coming by," said her father. "It means so much to my mother, especially since she can't get to church anymore."

"Hmm," said the minister. "There are people who want to and can't, and there are people who can but don't want to."

"Yes, well, that's the way it is," said Maria's father. "Shall I get your coat?"

"Yes, please."

"Enjoy the rest of your evening," said Maria's father.

"The same to you," said the minister, "and I look forward to greeting you in God's house one of these days."

The front door clicked shut. Maria heard her father walk back through the kitchen. She thought about what the minister had said about God's house. She never knew that God had a house. She listened to the slurping sound of the dishwater going down the drain.

Now daddy's emptying out the dishpan, she thought. In her head she watched the foaming water flowing through all sorts of twisting pipes until it reached the underground caverns beneath their house. All that water in her head made Maria have to pee. She got out of bed. The linoleum floor felt ice cold under her feet, which made her have to pee even more. She ran to the bathroom, but when she sat on the toilet only a few drops came out.

Maybe I only had to pee in my head, Maria thought as she flushed the toilet. Now don't start thinking about the toilet water flowing through all those slimy tunnels to a big lake under the city, Maria said severely to herself, or you'll just have to go again.

Returning from the bathroom, Maria saw that a light had been turned on in her bedroom. On the edge of her bed sat her father. Maria looked at his face. Luckily the anger was gone.

"Hop back in, eavesdropper," he said.

"I'll try not to do it ever again," said Maria. "You're not angry anymore?"

"I'm not angry anymore," said her father. He kissed her on the forehead. "Sleep well, now."

"What does God's house look like?" asked Maria as her father tucked her in tight.

Maria's father looked at her questioningly.

"That's what the minister said to you just before he

37

left. He was talking about God's house."

Her father frowned.

"I couldn't help it," said Maria. "I tried not to listen, but it didn't work. You were talking so loud."

Maria's father ran his hand lightly across her cheek. "Right," he said. "Give me a break. God's house is the church, Nosey Nellie."

"Does God live in the church with the minister?" asked Maria, sitting straight up in bed.

"From the way the minister talks you would almost think so, yes."

"Do you think so?"

"I don't think God has a house. I think God is a tramp who wanders around in people's heads. And wherever He goes He leaves all kinds of photos of Himself, and in every photo He looks different."

"Do you have a photo of God in your head?" asked Maria.

"When I was little I did, but when I got older I tore it up."

"Too bad," said Maria. She lay back down again and pulled up the blankets. "I'd really like to see God sometime."

Her father shrugged his shoulders. "Maybe it's better that you can't see Him. Then you can come up with your own idea of what He looks like. That's much more fun, don't you think?"

"Grandma listens to the word of God every Sunday on the radio. Have you ever heard God?"

"No."

"Me neither," said Maria. "Grandma never lets me listen. She says I can't sit still and that with me the word of God would just go in one ear and out the other anyway. Is that true?"

"Don't believe everything that grandma says," said her father. "And now get a good night's sleep. Tomorrow's another day full of questions." He bent down and gave Maria a kiss. "Goodnight, sweet Maria."

Maria's father walked out of her room, shut the door softly behind him, and walked down the stairs. Maria turned on her side and thought about God. She didn't want to come up with her own idea of God. She wanted a photo of God in her head, just like her father used to have.

It was Wednesday, twelve o'clock noon. Maria ran home. Luckily she didn't have school on Wednesday afternoons. The kitchen table was already set by the time she got there, and her mother was waiting for her. Maria threw her coat in the corner and tugged off her shoes. She quickly pulled up a chair and spread peanut butter on two slices of bread. After slapping the slices together, she pounded the sandwich twice with the palm of her hand.

"Is that necessary?" her mother asked.

"It goes down faster this way," said Maria.

"If I didn't know any better, I'd think you were raised by pigs."

Maria thought her mother was a nag. She crammed the sandwich into her mouth at top speed, jumped down from her chair, and went to put on her shoes and coat.

"Maria, your milk," her mother called. Maria

walked back to the table. Without bothering to sit down, she emptied the glass in one gulp.

"Bye, Mom. I'm going."

"Tell Grandma Bedstone I said hello."

"No," said Maria. "You don't even believe that Grandma Bedstone tells stories. So I'm not going to tell her you said hello." With that she slammed the door behind her. Running to the end of the street, she crept through the hole in the cemetery hedge. Grandma Bedstone's gravestone was under a big chestnut tree.

"Hi, Grandma Bedstone. It's me, Maria," said Maria after tapping on the stone three times.

Summer was almost over. On top of the gravestone lay the first chestnuts, gleaming in the sun. Maria stuffed them into the pockets of her coat. When she got home later she would make a whole zoo full of animals with the chestnuts and some wooden matches. Maybe Grandma Bedstone would like a few chestnuts, too, she thought. She dug a hole next to the gravestone with her hands and filled the hole with chestnuts. Then she covered the hole over with dirt.

"Now you can make animals, too, Grandma," said Maria.

"No, not animals," said grandma sleepily, and she yawned a great big yawn. "I'm going to make trees."

"Trees?" asked Maria. "That sounds like fun. I want to learn how to do that."

"Out of the question. That's not for little girls like you. Making trees is very difficult. And it takes a very long time. To do it you need all the time in the world, which you don't have and I do."

"What kind of trees will they be?" asked Maria.

"Come back in a few years and you'll find out," said Grandma Bedstone.

Grandma fell silent. Maria thought she could hear her quietly snoring under the stone. Grandma slept a great deal. That's because it was pitch dark under the ground, and you could never tell if your eyes were open or shut. And before you knew it you fell asleep. At least that's what always happened with Grandma Bedstone.

"Grandma, don't fall asleep just yet. I have to ask you something."

"What now?" grumbled grandma.

"Do you believe in God?"

"Are you crazy? Of course not."

"So you think God doesn't exist?"

"I think God is something that people bring on themselves."

Sometimes Grandma Bedstone said very complicated things, Maria thought. The next time she did a big cleanup in her head, this answer was sure to be right there on the pile of things she didn't understand.

Maria looked at the spiny green jackets on the ground that the gleaming chestnuts had pulled off. They hadn't even bothered to hang their jackets up, she thought. Just look at them lying around everywhere. Maria carefully picked one up. She ran her fingers along the spines and closed her eyes. Suddenly it had become a little porcupine. Maria heard a pigeon cooing in the branches overhead. She opened her eyes to try to see it, but the pigeon had hidden itself among the leaves, just as grandma lay hidden under the stone.

"Grandma," said Maria. "Grandma, listen."

"You listen to me," said grandma impatiently. "I'm not lying here just to chitchat. Leave me alone."

"I just want to know one thing. Then I'll go."

"All right, let's have it. And hurry up."

"Do you know daddy's mother?"

"That dragon, you mean?"

"I mean Grandma Forever."

"Isn't she pushing up the daisies yet, the old witch?"

"No, she's lying in her bed in our attic."

"Well, that's a fine state of affairs," said grandma.

"No it's not," said Maria. "With Grandma Forever

nothing's ever fine. Just when you think everything's fine she rings her bronze bell and she wants a glass of carrot juice or beet juice. Or she wants to know what time it is. Or what day it is. Or she says there's a hair in her brown rice and that it's my mother's. And then she pulls one of her own silver hairs out of the food. My mother doesn't even have silver hair."

"I get it. The dragon hasn't changed a bit."

Maria wondered if she dared ask Grandma Bedstone her question. She decided to go ahead and ask.

"May I bring Grandma Forever with me?"

"Where?"

"Here."

Maria waited for an answer, but there wasn't a sound to be heard.

"Grandma, I asked you something."

She pressed her ear up against the stone and listened to see if Grandma Bedstone was saying something, but nothing happened.

No news is good news, Maria said to herself.

She heard the rustle of leaves overhead. A gray pigeon flew away in the direction of Maria's house.

"Not by the hair on my chinny-chin-chin," said Grandma Forever, and she pulled her blanket up tight. Maria looked at grandma's chin. There must be one hair on that chin of hers that would agree, thought Maria. But grandma was stubborn. She looked straight ahead and didn't say a word.

"But you like to go for walks," said Maria, trying again.

"Not with you I don't."

"Why not?"

"Because you're a sassy monkey."

Maria wanted to put her hands under her armpits and screech "Ooh, ooh, ooh" real loud, but she stopped herself just in time. If she did that, grandma would wave her long, skinny finger in the air like a witch and start ranting and raving that the Lord would punish her. Even though Maria thought it was very funny, she knew that was no way to get grandma to go for a walk.

"Don't you want to visit Grandma Bedstone?" asked Maria.

"Grandma who?"

"Grandma Bedstone, mom's mother."

"Oh, her," said Grandma Forever, and she sniffed. "She's been dead for ages. Your mother is from weak stock, my dear. I hope for your sake you've got your father's blood in your veins, or you'll be kicking the bucket so fast you won't know what hit you."

"Grandma Bedstone isn't dead at all. Grandma Bedstone is asleep under a stone," said Maria.

"Get away with your fiddle-faddle."

"No, really."

"Well, why don't you wake up that miracle grandma of yours and bring her here?"

"I can't," sighed Maria. "She never goes to visit anyone. She's too old for that. But if you want, we can go and visit her. Or are you too old, too?"

"Too old?" snorted grandma. "I'm only ninety-three. And I don't give up without a fight." She threw off the blankets and sat up with a groan. Perched on the edge of her bed, she fished around with her toes for her slippers.

"Let's go. Give me a hand, sassy monkey. I'm going to show you what real walking is." Dressed in her pink nightgown, she leaned on Maria's arm and shuffled inch by inch to the old-fashioned wardrobe in the corner of the attic.

"What's the weather like outside?" grandma asked as she turned the key in the lock of the wardrobe's wooden door.

"Nice," said Maria. "The sun is shining, and there's no wind."

"I'm putting on a woolen dress anyway. If you're not careful you catch cold before you know it."

Maria looked at the long row of dresses hanging in grandma's closet. There must have been a hundred. So many dresses that nobody ever wore, just hanging there in the dark, bored stiff.

Grandma stuck her skinny arms up in the air.

"Hurry up. Don't just stand there. Pull off my nightgown. And be careful with my hair."

Maria stood on a chair, which made her quite a bit taller than grandma. Carefully she pulled the nightgown up over grandma's bent back. There stood grandma in her white undershirt and baggy underpants. The skin on grandma's arms and legs was as white as a blank sheet of paper in Maria's sketchbook. It looked as if someone had scratched a couple of thin blue stripes on her skin with a pen. Was it the strong blood from her father's side that was running through those stripes? Maria wondered. She jumped off the chair.

"What dress do you want to put on?" asked Maria.

"Quiet, child. I'm thinking." Grandma let her hand glide along the fabric of the dresses and came to a stop. "I wore this when your grandpa and I were married fifty years." Maria pulled the dress and its hanger out of the closet to get a better look. It was a dark blue dress with no decorations at all. Maria thought it was boring. But she decided not to say anything. If she did, she knew grandma would never agree to go for a walk.

"What do you think of this?" asked grandma.

"Pretty," said Maria with a straight face.

"I don't like it," said grandma. "It's boring. But your grandpa thought it was pretty, so I bought it. I haven't worn it once since that party."

Maria put the dress back in the closet.

"And this one?" she asked, pointing to a yellow summer dress.

Grandma took the dress out of the closet and began to laugh. The fabric was swarming with animals. Maria saw elephants, zebras, giraffes, lions, ostriches, flamingos, rhinoceroses, and hippopotamuses. The whole zoo was there on grandma's dress.

"I bought this when I was still a young girl. I was about fifty, I guess. Your grandpa always called it Noah's dress."

"And Noah was the boss of the zoo."

"No, dummy. Noah was the boss of the ark. Haven't your father and mother ever told you that story?"

Maria shook her head. Grandma hung Noah's dress back in the closet.

"What's to become of you?"

Maria didn't know.

"What dress do you want to put on?" asked Maria impatiently.

"Take it easy," said grandma. "Keep your shirt on. You've got to choose a dress with care. I choose a dress that suits the way I feel today."

"How do you feel today?"

"Appley," said grandma.

Maria was dying to know what that meant, appley, but what she really wanted was to go for a walk. So without asking any questions she pulled out a green dress with yellow apples on it and held it up in front of grandma's nose.

"Will this do?" she asked.

Grandma looked the dress up and down. She felt

the fabric.

"It's not wool," she said, "but it is appley and thick. Fine. It'll have to be this one."

Maria climbed back onto the chair. She let the apple dress slip over grandma's arms and head.

"Now a thick pair of pantyhose," said Maria, and she grabbed a pair from a drawer beneath the dresses. Grandma sat on the chair. Maria helped her pull up the pantyhose and put on her shoes.

"You look beautiful," said Maria when she was finished and grandma was standing up. Then grandma decided she wanted to put on her very thickest coat.

"Grandma, the sun is shining outside. It's not cold."

"It's almost October. Autumn is almost here. You've got to dress carefully."

Maria sighed.

"And that's going, too," said grandma, pointing to a red umbrella in the corner of the closet.

"Grandma, it's dry outside. What do we need an umbrella for?"

"That's not an umbrella. It's a parasol. An umbrella is for the rain. A parasol is for the sun. I don't want to suffer sunstroke."

Maria sighed once more.

"What are you doing, sighing like that?" asked grandma. "Don't you feel well, child?"

"I feel peary," muttered Maria.

"Don't mumble so. I can't understand you."

"I didn't say anything," said Maria, and she gave grandma her arm. "Okay, now we're going for a walk to visit Grandma Bedstone."

"Tell me the story of the boss of the ark?" Maria asked Grandma Forever when they were outside. Moving like a couple of snails, they inched their way slowly, arm in arm, down the street toward the cemetery. Grandma had to stop at every single flower, every plant, and every bush. If they kept this up, Maria thought, they'd still be walking by tomorrow morning.

"What kind of tree is this?" asked grandma.

Maria shrugged her shoulders.

"You don't know anything," said grandma. "This is a sycamore. You can tell it's a sycamore from the bark." Grandma pointed to the splotchy trunk of the tree. The bark was peeling off the trunk in big patches. It looked like a snake that was shedding its skin.

"Is it sick?" asked Maria.

"No, it's supposed to be like that."

Maria put her arm back through Grandma Forever's and walked quietly alongside her.

"Now tell me about that ark," she urged.

"Okay, okay," muttered grandma. "But first I have to sit down." Maria and grandma sat down side by side on a nearby wooden bench.

"One day God made it rain," began grandma. "Heavy drops started falling from dark clouds. It rained, and it rained, and it rained. At first the people thought it was just one of those days as far as the weather was concerned. They stayed inside and stared out their windows at the rain, which was coming down in buckets. But when a week had passed and it still hadn't stopped raining and the tables and chairs began floating through their living rooms, they began to get worried. They put on their raincoats and their rain pants, and they climbed up on the roofs of their houses. They shouted at the heavens that enough was enough, but their cries of distress were washed away by the raging waterfall from above. For forty days and forty nights, the clouds were squeezed out like sponges by an invisible hand. Finally there wasn't a drop more to be squeezed. All the clouds were wrung out and blown away before you could say Jack Robinson.

"Now the air was as dry as a bone, and the earth was soaked through and through. The world had turned into a watery planet, one big ocean without islands, without people, without animals, without plants, without trees, without flowers. Everything and everybody was dead – except Noah. He and his wife and his children and a whole menagerie had been saved by God. Noah had survived the flood by floating around on that huge ocean on a boat that he called an ark.

"Before the rains had begun Noah had spent months sawing and hammering on that boat. Even when everything was still fine and dandy, he was out there working on his ark like a demon. And the people laughed at him, because the ark got to be so big that it didn't fit anywhere. It didn't fit in the stream next to his house. It didn't fit in the lake outside town. There wasn't any water for miles around that could hold Noah's ship. It even got to be too big for Noah's imagination, but he kept on building because God had told him to. And when he was finally finished, he called his wife and children and told them to take a look.

"'Beautiful,' said his wife, and she gave Noah a proud pat on the back. Noah's children scowled at the huge hulk standing in the yard behind their house. That's some father we've got there, they thought, and went back to work.

"The next day Noah sent invitations all around the neighborhood to come to an ark open house. Everybody, young and old, rich and poor, was invited to see the work he had done. On the morning of the open house Noah got up early. When he opened the shutters in his bedroom he saw that the sky above the town was as black as tar. He hoped with all his heart that the festivities wouldn't be a total washout. Running to the ark, he grabbed the gangplank and put it in position. He waited an hour, but no one came. He waited another hour, but except for two dogs and two cats, who had slipped in when he wasn't looking, nobody showed any interest in his ark. Noah was disappointed. He looked up. A heavy raindrop had just fallen on his nose.

"'And now it's starting to rain,' he sighed.

"By the end of the day Noah was soaking wet. He shut the door of the ark and pulled out the gangplank. Then he walked slowly back to his house through the pouring rain.

"That night he didn't sleep well. There was thunder and lightning, and out in the backyard he thought he heard the mooing, roaring, bleating, and squawking of all kinds of animals. He gave his wife a nudge.

"'Do you hear that?' he asked.

"His wife rubbed her eyes sleepily and couldn't believe her ears.

"'Am I awake or asleep?' she asked.

"They walked outside in their pajamas. It was still raining, and the rain was up to their ankles. Next to the ark was a long row of animals waiting beneath the closed door, animals of every color, shape, and size. Some of them were animals that Noah knew by name. Others he had never seen before. Noah put the gangplank into position and opened the door of the ark.

"'Call the children,' he said to his wife. 'I don't like the looks of this.'

"Noah's wife ran off and came back with their sons, Shem, Ham, and Japheth. They had their wives with them. Still a little groggy from sleep, they hurried into the ark, stumbling over the chickens and geese that were crowding around the entrance. Noah stood next to the gangplank, wringing his hands.

"'I just hope they all fit,' he moaned.

"When the last animals were aboard and had found a place inside the ark, Noah himself stepped in. He pulled the gangplank inside, shut the door of the ark, and locked it. It wouldn't be long before the ark started floating. He always knew there had to be enough water somewhere to hold his ark."

Grandma was silent. Maria sighed.

"What a beautiful story," Maria said.

"It's not a beautiful story at all," said grandma as she rose from the bench with a groan. "It's a terrible story. All those people drowning in the sea because of the wrath of God. You call that a beautiful story?"

"Why did God flood the whole earth?"

"He was angry with the people."

"But why? What did they do wrong?"

"They were disobedient. And God doesn't like disobedient people. He also doesn't like disobedient children."

Just like Santa Claus, thought Maria.

Suddenly grandma broke wind right there in the street. It lasted a long time, and it sputtered and whistled like fireworks.

"Wow," said Maria in admiration. "You really know how to fart."

Grandma looked at her severely.

"Watch your language, child. A lady never farts. A lady has intestinal problems."

Grandma stopped at a loose paving stone that popped up when she stood on its edge.

"What's that?" Grandma pointed with her bony finger to a little plant with small purple flowers. It shot up between two paving stones.

"That," said Maria, "is a weed." She knew that for certain, because her father had just explained it to her when she was helping weed the garden. Those little flowers were weeds, and you could pull them up and throw them away.

"No it's not, dummy. This plant is called speed-well," grandma said.

"It is not. It's a weed," said Maria.

"Sassy monkey," said grandma, and she poked Maria's arm with the tip of her parasol.

"Ouch!" yelled Maria.

"Don't scream so loud, child," hissed Grandma Forever, "or I'll never come with you again to see that Grandma Bedstone of yours."

Maria bit her lip. She pulled grandma through the iron gate and into the cemetery. That was the cemetery's front door. The hole in the hedge was the back door, but grandma couldn't go in that way. She'd have to duck down very low, and Maria knew that grandma wouldn't be able to do that.

Maria looked at the big pillar that the cemetary gate was connected to. She read the words written on the pillar:

God will
bring with Jesus
those who have
fallen asleep
in him

"There under that tree is where Grandma Bedstone is sleeping," said Maria.

"That's where your grandma is resting," said Grandma Forever. "It's not a bed, it's a grave."

"Grandma Bedstone is asleep," said Maria.

"She's resting," said Grandma Forever, and she struck the ground with her parasol. "She's dead, and she's resting, so to speak."

Maria didn't say anything. Grandma pinched her lips together.

"What's the name of the tree hanging over the grave of that Grandma Bedstone of yours?" asked

Grandma Forever after a few minutes.

"I know that," said Maria. "It's a chestnut tree."

"Correct," said grandma.

Maria noticed the rusty color that was already beginning to form around the edges of the leaves. She ran ahead to Grandma Bedstone's gravestone under the chestnut tree and tapped three times.

"Hi, Grandma Bedstone," she whispered. "It's me, Maria. And I've got Grandma Forever with me."

Grandma Bedstone didn't answer. Maria sat down on the edge of the white stone and looked at Grandma Forever. Leaning on her parasol she slowly shuffled a little closer. A faint breeze began to blow, and the autumn leaves on the ground played tag on grandma's feet. Maria bent over. With her lips almost pressed against the stone she said softly, "You shouldn't always believe everything that Grandma Forever says. She's not completely normal."

"What's all that whispering?" asked Grandma Forever.

"I'm talking to Grandma Bedstone," said Maria.

Grandma Forever looked at the white marble stone that Grandma Bedstone was lying under.

"Have you ever talked to Grandma Bedstone?" asked Maria.

"I don't talk to the dead. And you shouldn't do it either. It's a sin."

"And before Grandma Bedstone went under the stone to sleep? Did you ever talk to her then?"

"Not then either. Your mother's mother was a heathen. I don't talk to heathens."

"Isn't a heathen something like an Indian or a pirate?" asked Maria.

"No, dummy. A heathen is someone who says that God doesn't exist. An atheist. And people who don't believe in God come to a bad end."

Maria stopped talking. She was reminded of Santa Claus again. He was someone else who you either believed in or you didn't. She hadn't believed in him for a long time. Her father and mother didn't either, but even so they always sang about him at Christmas. Would they come to a bad end, too? she wondered.

"Grandma? Was Santa Claus a brother of the God you listen to on the radio?"

"No, child. Believing in Santa Claus is a heathen custom. It's a sin."

"But if you believe in God, do you have a special day for Him, too, like a birthday?"

"God doesn't have birthdays. God was never born. God has always existed."

That's too bad for Him, thought Maria. Because if Grandma's God never had a birthday, He could never have parties, and He'd never get any presents, and His father and mother would never hang up decorations for Him, and He wouldn't get a cake, and He couldn't go around the classroom treating everybody to birthday candy. Now that's a sin!

"Doesn't your God have any brothers or sisters?" asked Maria.

"Child, don't ask such impudent questions. You can't compare God with people. He doesn't have any family."

"Do you have a photograph of God?"

"The God of Abraham, Isaac, and Jacob doesn't fit in a photograph. He's much too big."

"Is the God of Abraham, Isaac, and Jacob the same as your God?"

Grandma nodded.

"I know Jacob already, he's my friend. But who are the other two?

"Abraham, Isaac, and Jacob are the patriarchs of the Bible. And Jacob, your friend, has the same name as one of them."

Maria thought for a minute.

"How many gods are there anyway?"

"There are lots of gods, but there's only one true God," said grandma. "The rest are false gods."

Maria tried to imagine a false god. She saw before her a snarling monster with razor-sharp false teeth that flashed in the sky.

Grandma takes her false teeth out at night, Maria thought, but what do the false gods do with theirs?

"You ready to go home?" asked Maria. "Grandma Bedstone has to sleep, and if we stand here talking she might get angry."

"Don't worry," said Grandma Forever. "That Grandma Bedstone of yours will never wake up. Not in a million years."

Maria sat with her elbows on the kitchen table, cradling her head in her hands and furiously swinging her legs back and forth. Every now and then she kicked one of her shoes against the empty kitchen chair on the other side of the table.

"Maria, cut it out," said Maria's mother.

Maria stopped swinging her legs and began to drum on the tabletop with her fingers.

"Maria! I'm warning you. You're getting on my nerves. I've had it up to here with you."

"But I don't know what I should do my report on."

"Then do it on that kids' news program."

"Alice did that already."

"Then do it on planes."

"I don't like planes. And you can't take a plane to school."

"Then take a toy plane."

"It's not real."

"Well, then I can't help you. What did Jacob do it on?"

"Jacob did it on rabbits, and he took Rabbi with him, his black rabbit. But you won't let me have a rabbit. I can't have a dog. I can't have a cat. You won't let me have anything."

"Honey, I'm allergic to animal fur. You know that."

"So what."

"Maria, if you keep it up with this moaning and groaning you can go sit in your room until you're ready to behave yourself."

"I don't want to behave myself."

Maria's mother took a few big steps to the kitchen door and jerked it open. "If you don't want to behave yourself," she said angrily, pointing upstairs through the doorway with her finger, "then go straight to your room. You can moan and groan up there all you want."

Maria slowly got up from her chair. She shuffled leisurely past her mother and dragged herself up the stairs. When she reached her bedroom, she plopped down on her bed and sat with her back against the wall and her knees pulled up.

I hate mothers, and I hate reports, she thought. Everybody in the class had already given their report, except for her. Tomorrow it was her turn, but she still didn't know what to do it on. Most of the children had taken their pets to school and talked about them. Just before Deborah was supposed to give her report, her guinea pig had escaped and hid behind the cabinet. Alex's turtle was shy and wouldn't come out of his house. Tim's dog was so nervous that he peed against the leg of the teacher's chair. Now those reports had really been good, Maria thought. Her report would have to be even better. She would have to take something very special. But what?

Maria heard her grandma sneeze explosively three times. Grandma's sneeze could wake the dead. Sometimes when she sneezed in the middle of the night, everybody in the house would sit bolt upright in bed in a state of shock.

Suddenly Maria sprang to her feet. She had an idea. She raced up to the attic two steps at a time and flew into grandma's room without knocking.

"Grandma, Grandma, listen," she shouted wildly. "Grandma, I'm going to give my report on you. Can I take you to school with me?"

"You're supposed to knock first before you come in, sassy monkey." Maria ran out of the room, shut the door, and knocked politely.

"Yes, come in. It's too late now," snarled grandma. "What do you want?"

"Can I please take you to school? I want to do my class report on you. Oh, please? Can I? Please?" Maria begged. "I'll never be fresh again. I'll always knock politely and always mind my p's and q's."

"What do I have to do?" asked grandma.

"Nothing," said Maria. "Just sit in front of the blackboard. And I'll talk about your life."

"That would take a week," said grandma.

"No, I can only talk for ten minutes. And then the children in the class are allowed to ask questions."

"Who do they ask?" asked grandma. "Me?"

"No, me. It's my report."

"I'll go only if I can say something, too," insisted grandma.

Maria thought for a minute. She knew that if she said no, grandma would clamp her lips together and not say another word. And that would be the end of her great plan.

"Agreed," said Maria, grabbing grandma's hand and shaking it solemnly.

"Keep your bacteria to yourself, sassy monkey," she said, wiping her hand off on the blanket. "Your hands are all sticky. Don't you ever wash them?"

Only when I've touched you, Maria wanted to say, but she swallowed her words just in time.

The next day Maria was standing in front of her class. Grandma Forever sat beside her on a chair. She held her pocketbook on her lap, clutching it with both hands. She was still wearing the fur coat she had put on in the attic, and she refused to take it off in Maria's classroom.

"It'll get stolen," she had said. Maria had done everything she could to talk grandma into wearing a different coat, but grandma had held her ground.

"It's almost winter, and in the winter a lady always wears a fur coat."

"Grandma, fur coats are mean. Fur coats are made of dead animals. You just don't wear something like that," Maria said.

"Nonsense," said grandma. "I'll wear what I want. There's nothing wrong with fur. Those animals are better off in my coat than in the wild. Take it from me."

Maria even went down on her knees in front of her

grandma and begged her to wear another coat, just this once. Grandma wouldn't dream of it.

"Stand up, foolish child. If I can't wear my fur coat, I'm not going."

Maria looked at the faces of the children in the class. They all stared at the old woman sitting on the chair in front of the blackboard. Grandma's silver hair was tied up in a knot. It glistened in the sun.

"Maria, you may begin," said the teacher.

Maria unfolded the piece of paper on which she had written her report.

"I don't have a pet," she said, "because my mother's allergic. But I do have a grandma, and she lives in the attic of my house. That's why I brought her along. My grandma is very old. She's ninety-three. She was born on a farm. She had a brother and three sisters. There were all kinds of animals on the farm: cows, pigs, and chickens. My grandma had to milk the cows and feed the chickens. When she went to school she had to walk very far. She wore wooden shoes because they lived on a farm. And when it froze in the wintertime she skated to school on the canals. My grandma's father and mother were very poor. They didn't even have a TV."

"Of course not, dummy," said Grandma Forever

loudly so everyone could hear. "That devilish contraption didn't even exist then."

Maria looked up from her paper. The children in the class began laughing and talking amongst themselves. The teacher told them all to be quiet so Maria could continue.

"When my grandma was as old as our teacher, she taught school, too. That's where my grandpa worked. And then they fell in love, and then they got married. And then grandma had a baby, and then she didn't want to be a teacher anymore."

"I wanted to," said Grandma Forever, interrupting Maria again, "but your grandpa wouldn't let me."

"Grandma, this is my report," said Maria. "You can't keep breaking in on me. Pets don't do that."

Grandma grew red with anger. "Sassy monkey," she shouted, and she tried to get out of her chair. The teacher stood up.

"When Maria is finished with her story," she said to Grandma Forever, "you and Maria can answer the children's questions together. How would that be?"

Grandma mumbled something no one could hear and dropped back into her chair.

"Maria, you may continue with your report," said the teacher.

"Grandma has eleven children. My father was the youngest. He didn't want to be born in the regular way, and so they took a knife and made a hole in my grandma's belly. That's called a cesarean section, and then they pulled my father out. You can still see the cut on grandma's belly. It's called a scar. Just like with the pirates." Maria paused a moment and looked at the teacher.

"Can grandma show us her scar?" she asked.

"Maybe that's not such a good idea, Maria," said the teacher. "Your grandma is sitting so nice and warm in her coat. Otherwise she might catch cold."

But Grandma Forever was already unbuttoning her fur coat. "I'd be happy to show off my belly," she said graciously.

"That's very nice of you," said the teacher, "but it's really not necessary. We believe you. Maria, you can continue."

"Grandma Forever didn't always live with us in the attic. First she lived with Grandpa Forever. But he's sleeping under a stone now in a cemetery on the other side of town. Grandma lies in bed all day. She listens to the words of the God of Abraham, Isaac, and Jacob on the radio. Those are the three patriarchs from the Bible, and my friend Jacob has the same name as one of them."

Maria looked up at Jacob and winked at him. Jacob's cheeks turned bright red. Maria kept on talking.

"The God of the patriarchs is grandma's God, too. My grandma says there are lots of other gods, but they're all as false as false teeth. Sometimes grandma listens to the minister when he talks on the radio, or she listens to the man who does the news, or to the orchestra.

"Grandma also sleeps a lot, and she's on a Moerman diet. That means eating special food, because she thinks she has cancer."

"I don't think I have cancer. I know I have cancer, but they're not going to stuff me in a coffin and put me in a hole in the ground," grandma muttered. Maria gave her grandma a withering look.

"Every day grandma reads the Bible. That's a book with exciting stories about her God. Grandma knows them all by heart. Sometimes the minister comes to see her. Not the one from the radio but the one from the church. And sometimes she goes for walks, but not very often. My grandma knows everything about trees and plants and about God."

Maria folded up her report.

"That was my report on my grandma."

"Thank you, Maria," said the teacher. "Who has

any questions?"

Jacob raised his hand.

"Go ahead, Jacob," said the teacher.

"Why does your grandma live with you in the attic and not in an old-people's home?"

"Your rabbit doesn't live in an old-people's home, does he?" said Maria.

The children in the class giggled quietly.

"Do you have to feed your grandma every day?" asked Deborah. The children began to laugh harder.

"No, my grandma isn't a guinea pig. My grandma doesn't get animal feed, she gets food." Now the class was roaring with laughter.

"Do you have to let your grandma out?" asked Tim. He had to scream to be heard above all the commotion.

"No, grandma goes on the potty," Maria screamed back.

Grandma stared straight ahead. The teacher looked at the class sternly. She clapped her hands and waited until it was completely quiet. "Shall we try to ask normal questions?" she said when everyone had finally quieted down. "Maybe someone has a question for Maria's grandma?"

Brendan raised his hand.

"Is your fur coat real fur?"

"No," shouted Maria at the top of her voice.

"You bet it is," said grandma, and she gave Maria a push.

"That's not true," said Maria. "It's fake fur."

"Maria, Brendan was talking to your grandma, not to you," said the teacher. "Let your grandma talk."

"It's not fake at all. This coat is made of the finest mink," said grandma. "They don't make them like this nowadays."

"But fur is really bad for the environment," said Brendan.

"You know what's bad for the environment?" asked grandma, and she looked around the classroom with fire in her eyes. "Sassy monkeys, that's what's bad for the environment. That's what they should make fur coats from, sassy monkey fur."

Maria looked at Brendan. She saw his lower lip begin to tremble.

"I don't think your grandma is nice at all," he said with a quavering voice.

"Neither do I," said Maria. Then the bell rang. All the children ran outside.

"Sassy monkeys," Grandma Forever called after them.

"You ruined my whole report with that stupid fur coat. Now all the kids are going to laugh at me," said

Maria, glaring at her grandmother with rage. "You can't be my grandma anymore. I want another grandma, a fake grandma with a fake fur coat." Maria ran out of the classroom after the other children.

"The Lord will punish you," Grandma Forever screamed at her.

"Maria, you're forgetting your grandma," called the teacher.

"She's not my grandma anymore," shouted Maria in reply, and she slammed the door with a bang.

Grandma didn't want Maria to come up to the attic anymore. She was very angry with her, and she wanted Maria to apologize. But Maria refused. It was all grandma's fault. She was the one who had to wear that stupid fur coat.

Maria lay on her back, staring into the darkness. She was very sad. If only she could crawl into her comfort hammock in the attic, then the sadness would go away. But she couldn't. The hammock had been stored in the shed when grandma came to live in the attic.

She looked at the glowing numbers of the clock radio on the nightstand. It was already three o'clock in the morning. Her father and mother had gone to bed a long time ago. Maria had heard them talking for a while in the bedroom next to hers. She couldn't understand what they were saying, but every now and then Maria could hear them laughing quietly. Now it was silent again in the house, and it had been for a long time.

Maria turned from her back to her side. She wished it was morning. There was a slit in the curtains, and the moon was shining right on her face. Maria threw off the covers and got out of bed. She walked to the window and opened the curtains. The dark trees with their bare branches stood there deathly still, just like skeletons. On the garden path below Maria saw her red ball gleaming in the moonlight. Suddenly she heard a strange noise. Maria pricked up her ears. It sounded like music, and it came from upstairs.

Very quietly she opened her bedroom door and crept up the stairway. The attic door was open a crack. Maria looked inside. Grandma was sitting up in bed and singing a song. There was light from the wall lamp above her head. On grandma's lap was a little black book with thin pages that rustled when grandma turned them with her long, skinny fingers.

Maria didn't recognize the song grandma was singing. It was about some animal being chased by hunters. Luckily the animal escaped. But all that running had made it thirsty, and now it was looking for water, the poor thing, and for God. Maria thought it was a beautiful song. Without even thinking, she pushed open the attic door. Grandma immediately stopped her singing.

"What do you want, sassy monkey?" she asked with a grumpy voice. "Don't you know what time it is?"

"I was awake, and I heard singing," said Maria, "and then I wanted to know where it was coming from."

Grandma looked at Maria with dark eyes.

"You're not allowed to prowl around the house so late at night," said grandma. "And you're not welcome in my attic at all."

"But you were singing so nicely," said Maria. "That's why I came. What are you singing?"

"Psalms," said grandma.

"What are they?"

"Those are songs King David wrote."

"They have a queen in England, but they don't have a king," said Maria.

"I know that, dummy," said grandma. "King David lived a long, long time ago. And he wasn't the king of England but of Israel."

"Is David a fairy-tale king?"

"No, of course not," said Grandma Forever impatiently. "Fairy tales are sinful. The story of King David is in the Bible."

"Will you tell me the story of King David?"

"Absolutely not," said grandma. "You have to go to bed."

"But I can't sleep."

Grandma stared straight ahead.

"What do you want to hear? Do you want to hear about how David slew the giant?"

Maria nodded.

"Fluff up my pillows first," said grandma. Maria grabbed the pillows behind grandma's back and gave them a good shake.

"There, that's better," said grandma. Maria sat down on the stool next to grandma's bed.

"It was a long time ago," grandma began. "Before King David was king of Israel there was a giant. The giant's name was Goliath. He was a soldier in the army of the enemy, the terrible Philistines. And that giant was so incredibly tall that he walked around all day with his head in the clouds. He was just as tall as the tales he told, and they were pretty tall. For instance, he said that he could wipe the army of Israel off the battlefield with the pinky of one hand. It was an awfully tall tale, but the warriors of Israel didn't doubt it for one second. They were scared stiff, just like Saul, who was king of Israel at the time. All day long, Goliath walked back and forth across the battlefield.

"'Nobody is as strong as I am, or as tall as me and my tales,' he shouted. 'Who dares to take me on, the great Goliath?'

"Every time Goliath finished with his roaring there wasn't a single sound on the battlefield. Nobody dared stand up to the blustering giant. All the Philistines in the enemy camp laughed and celebrated. Nobody was as strong and as tall as their hero. But one day, after Goliath had spent some time flexing his muscles and showing off his strength, it wasn't quiet anymore for a change. 'My tale is much taller than yours,' said a young man with red hair and freckles. He didn't even come up to Goliath's knees, so it took awhile before the giant was able to focus on him.

"'What did you say, you miserable mouse?' asked Goliath scornfully, and he bent over to get a look at the red-haired boy. He wasn't even a soldier. Goliath could see that quick as a wink. He didn't have any armor, and he didn't have a helmet, and he walked around on bare feet like a beggar. The only weapon he had was the slingshot in his hand.

"'I said my tale is much taller than yours,' the boy said to Goliath once more.

"'What's your name, you pathetic worm?'

"'David.'

"'Let's hear your tale, David, hero without socks,' sneered the giant.

"'Do you know the tale of the bare-footed hero who slew the giant?' asked the boy.

"'Don't make me laugh,' roared the giant.

"'Pardon me,' answered the boy. 'It certainly wasn't my intention to make you laugh.'

"Goliath looked at him for a while, speechless.

"'And how do you think you're going to slay me?' he asked.

"'With this slingshot and this stone.'

"'Over my dead body,' said the giant.

"'Well, you asked for it,' said the boy, and he whipped his slingshot around as fast as he could. The stone flew out and sailed through the air, and the giant fell flat on the ground."

Grandma Forever stopped talking. Maria looked at her in expectation.

"And then?" asked Maria.

"And then nothing," said grandma. "And then you went to bed."

"But how did David become king?"

"That's a long story. I'll tell you some other time. Now clear out. I want to sleep."

Maria stood up. Her feet were ice cold, even colder than the stone that Grandma Bedstone slept under. She gave grandma a kiss.

"Wait a minute," said grandma, and she put her hands in her lap.

"Do you see the palms of my hands, Maria?" she asked.

Maria nodded.

"You see the letters?" Maria bent over grandma's hands, but she didn't see anything.

"What letters, grandma?"

"Just follow the lines," she said, and she took Maria's right hand. With Maria's index finger she traced the lines in her own palm.

"An M, Maria. You see the capital letter M in my one hand and another M in the other?" Maria looked at the thin red lines in her grandma's palms. Suddenly she saw the letters.

"Those two letters stand for two words, Maria. Foreign words from Latin. That's an old language that's almost never spoken anymore. *Memento Mori*— that's what those letters stand for."

"What does that mean, Grandma?"

"That means, remember you must die. In other words, don't forget that the day of your death is coming."

Maria thought about this a moment. She looked at her own hands. She saw that she had two M's, too.

Then she turned her hands to the outside.

"Grandma, I don't think it's the letter M. If you turn your hands around it's the letter W. Two W's. Look." Maria showed her hands to her grandma.

Grandma looked at Maria's turned palms. "And what are those two W's supposed to mean, smarty-pants?" asked grandma.

"Wake up, Wake up," said Maria. "Those two W's mean Wake up."

Grandma looked at Maria with glistening eyes.

"Hurry up, now," she said, and pushed Maria away. "To bed with you."

Maria walked to the door and turned around.

"Grandma."

"What now?"

"I don't need a fake grandma with a fake fur coat. I want a real grandma. Will you be my grandma again?"

"There's no wanting about it, whippersnapper. I am your grandma, whether you like it or not. That's the way it's always been and the way it will always be. All you have to do is join in. Goodnight."

Gradually Maria woke up. What time was it anyway? she wondered. She looked at the numbers on the clock radio. Ten o'clock! She sprang out of bed. It was much too late. School had started a long time ago. Why hadn't her mother called her? Maria ran downstairs in her pajamas. Her father was sitting in the kitchen in his bathrobe, leisurely reading the newspaper.

"Do you know what time it is?" asked Maria.

"I sure do," answered her father, looking at the kitchen clock. "It's just past ten. Did you sleep well?"

"Don't you have to go to work?" asked Maria.

"No, scatterbrain. It's Saturday."

Maria slapped herself on the forehead. "I completely forgot," she said. "I thought I had to go to school."

"Nope. You've got the day off. Why don't you go outside and play with Jacob?" her father asked.

"Can't," said Maria. "Jacob isn't home. He spent the night at his grandma's."

"Lucky Jacob."

"Can I spend the night with Grandma Bedstone sometime?"

"I don't think it's such a good idea to stay overnight in a cemetery, Maria."

"Could I spend the night with Grandma Forever in the attic?"

"First you have to tell grandma you're sorry."

"I'm not telling her I'm sorry. Grandma shouldn't have acted so stupid."

"It's really your own fault, Maria. You know grandma always does and says strange things. You shouldn't have taken her to school. Your mother and I warned you, but you just wouldn't listen."

"Grandma shouldn't have put on that idiotic fur coat. Then nothing would have happened."

"Honey, your grandma isn't a Barbie doll that you can dress and undress any way you want."

Maria didn't say anything.

"Well then, why don't you take grandma's breakfast upstairs? She hasn't rung her bell yet, but I think any minute now she'll want something to eat. Then you can empty grandma's potty and make up at the same time."

"I already did that last night," said Maria.

Her father looked her questioningly.

"You emptied grandma's potty last night?"

"No, silly. I couldn't sleep, and then I heard grandma singing in the attic, so I went to see what she was doing, and then we made up."

"But you didn't say you were sorry?"

"No, I asked if she would be my grandma again."

"Very good."

Maria's father slipped back behind his newspaper.

"Do you know how David got to be king?" asked Maria as she made herself a jam sandwich.

"Which David?"

"The David who slew Goliath."

"Oh, him. I'm not so good at telling those stories. Your grandma is the expert, honey. Hurry and take up her breakfast. And ask about spending the night with her while you're at it."

Maria nodded. She walked up the two sets of stairs with the heavy tray. When she reached the attic she tapped softly on the door with her foot. It was quiet on the other side.

Maria waited a minute and put the tray on the floor. She made a fist and knocked three times on grandma's wooden door.

"Grandma. It's me, Maria."

Grandma still didn't reply. Carefully Maria opened the door. She stepped inside and put the breakfast on the stool next to grandma's bed. Grandma was still asleep. Her mouth was wide open.

"Grandma, listen," whispered Maria softly into grandma's ear. "It's after ten o'clock. Your breakfast is ready."

Grandma didn't budge. She just kept on sleeping. Maria looked at her snow-white face. It looked like marble. Maria placed a little kiss on grandma's cheek. Her cheek was hard and cold. Maria felt a shiver go through her body. She gently shook grandma's arm, which was lying on the checkered blanket. The arm was stiff. She looked at grandma's hands. She looked at her own hands.

"Wake up," said Maria out loud. "Grandma, wake up now. You have to tell me how David got to be king, and if I can spend the night with you."

Grandma was silent.

Slowly Maria walked down the two sets of stairs. She stood in the kitchen doorway.

"Daddy," she said, "Grandma won't wake up."

14

The organ in God's house was playing a melody. Maria listened. She knew that tune. It was the psalm of King David – the psalm that grandma had sung the night Maria couldn't sleep, the song about the animal searching for water.

Maria looked all around. The house of God was big and high. The windows were colored, and copper candelabras hung overhead from the ceiling. Little lights were shining from each one. Maria sat on a wooden pew in the first row, between her father and her mother. All her uncles and aunts were in the same row. Behind her, among the big round pillars, she saw lots of serious faces. Jacob, her friend, was there, too, with his father and mother. He waved to her. Maria waved back.

She looked up at her father's face. He seemed a little sad. Maria put her hand on his hand. He looked at her and smiled. Then he looked straight ahead at the stopped. The pillars looked like the big trunks of the trees in the cemetery where Grandma Bedstone was sleeping, except these trunks were made of stone, and they didn't have any branches or leaves. The minister bowed his head and folded his hands. He stood there for a long time. It was so quiet in the church you could hear a pin drop. Then the minister climbed the stairs. He walked through a little doorway and ended up on a wooden balcony that was attached to the stone tree trunk. That way everybody in the church could easily see him.

"Why's he standing there?" Maria quietly asked her father.

"That's the pulpit," said her father. "That's where ministers always do their talking."

"We are gathered here together ... ether ... ether," echoed the minister, "to carry Nelly Maria Elizabeth van Dalen ... alen ... alen to her grave ... ave ... ave."

The minister spoke slowly and seriously. The church was filled with echoes. Each word that the minister said bounced back and forth off the walls. He was talking about grandma, about Grandma Forever who suddenly had so many names.

"Her earthly life has come to an end ... end ... end. Her step will no longer be heard in the streets ... eets

... eets, nor her voice in the marketplace ... ace ... ace. We mourn this loss ... oss ... oss. At the same time, we are aware of our own weakness ... ness ... ness. For this life is but a breath ... eath ... eath, and we, too, will have to appear one day ... ay ... ay before the throne of the God of wrath ... ath ... ath."

Maria tried to listen to the minister, but his words tumbled over each other and made her dizzy. It was as if her ears were cross-eyed so that she heard everything three times. The church was a big, echoing well, she imagined, and at the bottom of the well was God, sitting there like a parrot, repeating all the minister's words.

"Brothers and sisters ... isters ... isters. Keep your lamps lit ... lit ... lit. Be on guard like the wise virgins ... irgins ... irgins. No one knows ... ows ... ows if he will be given entrance to the golden city ... ity ... ity. Neither do we know for sure ... ure ... ure if Maria van Dalen ... alen ... alen has been received into the New Jerusalem ... alem ... alem or lost to eternal destruction ... uction ... uction.

Maria thought the minister was saying weird things. Of course Grandma Forever wasn't going to a golden city or to the new Jerusalem, and she wasn't going to get lost in Eternal Destruction, wherever that

"It used to be. But not anymore."

"But your grandma's dead, isn't she?"

"She's not dead. She's asleep."

The orchestra started playing more quietly. Maria turned up the radio. The orchestra played even more quietly. Maria turned the radio up even louder. Now the orchestra stopped playing altogether. It was silent in the radio. Maria turned all the knobs, but no more sound came out. Maybe the orchestra didn't want to play for her anymore, she thought. Maybe the orchestra only wanted to play for Grandma Forever. The man who did the news didn't say anything either. The minister was silent, so none of the words of God came out of the radio. Grandma probably should have taken the radio with her in the coffin.

Maria thought for a minute. She jumped out of the rocking chair and ran down the stairs to her own room with the radio under her arm. In the middle of all the junk on the top shelf of her closet she found a small red plastic shovel. She put the shovel and the radio in her backpack. Then she went downstairs and put on her coat.

"Where are you going?" asked her mother.

"To see Grandma Bedstone," said Maria.

"But why are you taking your backpack?"

was. Grandma Forever was going to the big cemetery at the other end of town. She was going to sleep there under the stone with Grandpa Forever. That's what her father had told her that morning. Maria raised her hand, just like at school when she wanted to say something or ask a question. Her mother pulled her arm down.

"What is it, Maria?" she asked quietly. "Do you have to go to the bathroom?"

"No," said Maria, "I have to ask the minister something."

"Not now, honey," said Maria's mother. "The minister is preaching his sermon."

But Maria wanted to say something now. What if the minister had mixed grandma up with somebody else's grandma? What if he started to say even more things about Grandma Forever that weren't right?

"Reverend," said Maria out loud. The minister had just taken a sip of water from the glass that stood on the edge of the wooden balcony. He swallowed the wrong way and began to cough.

"Reverend ... end ... end." Even Maria's words repeated themselves through the church. They bounced and tumbled through the minister's coughing. "Grandma's not going to a golden city ... ity ... ity.

Grandma's going to the other end of town ... own ... own to be with Grandpa Forever ... ever ... ever."

There was whispering in the church. Maria's mother gave her a poke with her elbow. Her father choked on the peppermint that Maria's mother had just given him. He began to gasp and cough, just like the minister. The minister shuffled a bit through the papers he had lying before him.

"Amen ... amen ... amen," said the minister, and the organ began to play.

Maria sat in the rocking chair in the attic, listening to grandma's radio. Her father had given it to her the day after grandma's funeral. "In memory of Grandma Forever," he had said.

It was still winter back then, but now spring had come again. Maria looked outside through the attic window. She heard a blackbird singing. The orchestra on the radio played the harmony. Would the musicians know that grandma wasn't living in the attic anymore? she wondered. Maria thought the music sounded sad. She felt sad, too. She missed grandma. The attic was so empty without her. Yesterday she had had an argument with Jacob about it. He had asked when they could play pirate in the attic again, and Maria had gotten very angry with him.

"We can't just start playing pirate in the attic," she had said. "It's grandma's attic."

"I thought it was your attic."

"Grandma's radio is in it. I'm going to listen to Grandma Forever's radio with Grandma Bedstone."

"I didn't know Grandma Bedstone liked that sort of thing."

"You know now," said Maria, and she stepped outside.

"Sassy monkey," said her mother.

"You're not allowed to say that," said Maria. "Only Grandma Forever can say that."

When Maria got to the alley behind the house she took to her heels. But she wasn't going to visit Grandma Bedstone. She ran until she had disappeared around the corner, then she crossed the big main road. She walked to the intersection where the traffic lights were. There she turned left and came to a wide street with high buildings on both sides.

Daddy works somewhere around here, Maria thought. She moved along the walls of the buildings like a nervous cat. It wasn't raining, and it wasn't cold, yet Maria pulled up her hood. She wanted to be sure her father wouldn't be able to spot her if he just happened to be looking out of his office window.

First she had to walk all the way down the long road that ran past the train station. That was the way she always went to school. When she got to the house of God she had to turn right. Maria started wondering whether she knew the rest of the way.

She walked through an avenue of red beeches and ran her hand along the smooth bark of the trees. This avenue was familiar. She had been here the day of Grandma Forever's funeral. She had sat between her father and mother on the backseat of a big black car with gray curtains. It was cold outside then. The trees shivered in the rain and wind. Maria had tried to count the drops on the window, but it hadn't worked. There were so many, and they wouldn't keep still. They kept rolling down, like tears.

But today it was dry. The sun was shining, and Maria got so warm that she took off her coat. She tied the sleeves around her waist and looked at the fresh little leaves on the branches of the beech trees. They were so new they gleamed.

Isn't that strange, thought Maria. In the winter people walk around in their heavy coats, while the trees stand there half frozen with nothing on at all, stark naked. But in the spring when it gets warm – that's when the trees put on their leaves, just when the people are going outside without coats.

Maria was getting tired, and she looked at her watch. She had been walking half an hour. Her legs hurt. Did she still have far to go, and was this really the right way? An old lady came along, dressed all in pink. She looks just like a walking candy cane, thought Maria. Even her hair had a pink glow to it. At the end of a pink leash she was walking a small, white, furry dog. The dog looked like the white ball of wool that her mother was knitting a sweater from. But this ball had legs and a pink bow. The ball of wool sniffed at Maria's feet. The walking candy cane came to a stop.

"May I pet him?" asked Maria.

"Wherever did you get that idea?" said the pink woman. "She's not wet. She's nice and dry and clean. I take good care of her."

Maria looked at the woman as if she were crazy.

"I asked if I could pet him," said Maria.

"Oh, pet. You said 'pet.' Of course you may. I thought you said 'wet.' I'm a little deaf, you see. You have to speak up when you talk to me."

Maria crouched down to pet the dog.

"What's his name?" she shouted up to the woman.

"Her name is Tootsie. It's a girl. And what's your name?"

"Maria," Maria shouted. "And I'm a girl, too."

"I thought so," said the woman.

"My mother won't let me have a dog," said Maria,

"or a rabbit. No animals at all. They make her sneeze."

"What are you talking about, my dear? It's not going to freeze. It's the end of April. Summer's on the way."

Tootsie had had enough of Maria's petting. She began pulling on her pink leash and yapping.

"Toot-toot-tootsie good-bye," said the woman.

"Is this the way to the cemetery?" asked Maria quickly, before the pink woman could walk any farther. She pointed to the park in front of them.

"If you walk through the park, you'll come to a big traffic circle. At that circle is a rosarium ..."

"A what?"

"A rosarium. It's a lovely garden with all kinds of roses, but they're not blooming yet. It's too early in the season. You should come back in the summer to take a look."

Maria nodded.

"But to get to the cemetery you have to walk through the rosarium. Then cross the street, and you'll see a wooden flower stand in the distance. It's just across from that stand. A big green wrought iron gate. Can't miss it."

"Thank you," said Maria.

"You're welcome, Maria. It was nice meeting you."

Maria walked through the green wrought iron gate across from the flower stand, then down an avenue of old trees. She didn't know what kind of trees they were. Grandma Forever would have known their names.

At the end of the avenue was a red brick building with a clock tower. Maria saw that it was two-thirty. On the lawn in front of the building was a small pond with water splashing from a fountain. Next to the fountain was a statue of a black woman in a white dress. The woman stared into the water of the pond. Maria stopped and looked around her. Where had they buried grandma that winter, anyway? It was in an avenue with sycamore trees, that she could still remember.

A fat man came walking by. He wore a gray suit with white stripes, and there was a cigar sticking out of his mouth. His cheeks hung down like deflated balloons, and his nose looked like an electric socket. Just like a dressed-up pig, Maria thought. The pig almost ran Maria over without noticing her. He didn't even see her standing there.

"Do we have enough cake?" he asked another man who was standing behind Maria.

"Enough for a whole orphanage."

The fat man drew on his cigar and blew out a big cloud of smoke. It smelled horrible, Maria thought.

"Sir," asked Maria, "are you the boss of the cemetery?"

The fat man looked down absentmindedly.

"Why?" he asked.

"I'm looking for the road with the sycamores."

"The road with what?"

"The sycamores. My grandma is sleeping under them."

"It's a kind of tree," said the other man, who had come to stand next to them. "The sycamores are there to the left," he said to Maria. "If you walk down that path you'll run right into them." He pointed out the way.

"There must be lots of ministers coming here to visit," said Maria.

The two men frowned.

"You should give ministers a thick slice of cake and not any dried-up old cookies, but if there are cupcakes in the pot that's okay, too," said Maria as she turned around. She walked past a white painted wooden fence and came to a gravel walk. The gravel crunched under her feet. Everywhere she looked she saw big rectangular gravestones. Some were lying on the ground, and others were standing straight up. Some of the stones were beautifully decorated with flowers or angels. Maria read the names on the stones. She knew that those were the names of the people who had been buried and were now sleeping under their stones. A cemetery is really a kind of underground city of sleep, Maria thought.

A shadow fell across the path. It came from the big chestnut trees growing there. She looked at the green foliage over her head. Not a single strip of sun shone through. Maria noticed that the chestnut tree was in bloom. Candles was what Grandma Forever called those plumes with the white blossoms. Suddenly Maria saw a small purple flower growing between the gravestones. If that isn't a weed, thought Maria, then I don't know what is. She chuckled to herself and bent down to pick the flower for Grandma Forever.

A little farther on was a black gravestone gleaming on the ground. At the top of the stone Maria saw a picture of a white horse with four riders.

Those with faith never hasten, it said.

If you're sleeping in a grave there's nothing to hasten about anyway, thought Maria. She strolled along peacefully. At the end of the path was a small green container with withered flowers sticking out of it. And next to that was a pump with iron sprinklers that swayed back and forth quietly in the wind.

Maria turned onto the next path. Halfway down, near a big pile of sand, was a man at work. He was pulling flowers and wreaths out of a deep hole in the ground. Maria walked toward him cautiously. She looked in the hole and saw a wooden coffin. The man bent down and picked up a bunch of white tulips and a long red rose.

Then he began shoveling sand. The falling sand hit the lid of the coffin with little thuds.

"Is that your grandma?" Maria asked, pointing to the pit.

The man looked up for a moment and went back to shoveling.

"Nope," he said. "My grandma is still alive and kicking. It'll be a long time before she's six feet under." A cigarette was hanging from his lips. Sweat dripped from his face. Gradually the mountain of sand disappeared into the hole in the ground. Maria couldn't see the coffin at all anymore.

"Whose grandma is that then?"

"No idea."

The man tossed his shovel on the ground and laid a wide wooden board over the sand.

"Is that a door?" asked Maria.

"Are you kidding? That's just a board."

"Doesn't this grandma get a stone?"

The man stood with his hands on his hips and looked at Maria.

"Say, what are you doing here anyway?" he asked. "This is no place for little kids."

"Why not?" asked Maria. "I can come to see my grandma, can't I?"

"Is your grandma buried here?"

Maria nodded.

"She's sleeping under a stone near the sycamores."

"Oh," said the man with a smile. "That's a nice cozy spot for lying down. And now you're going to go tuck her in?

"Don't have to," said Maria. "Grandma Forever was tucked in awhile ago, and she's been sleeping under the ground all winter long."

"Then I'll make sure I walk on my tiptoes," said the man. "Otherwise she might wake up."

"You do that," said Maria. The man shook his head with a laugh and went back to work. Maria decided she had stood there long enough and continued on her way. "Bye-bye," she said as she left.

Behind a tall hedge she saw the sycamores in the distance. Grandma Forever must be lying around there somewhere, she thought. Before turning onto a side path she looked back at the man for a moment. All the wreaths and flowers that he had first taken from the coffin he now carefully placed on the board over the grave.

Maria let her backpack slide off. It was so warm that her shirt clung to her back. Next to which sycamore did we bury grandma anyway? she wondered. Wasn't it the eighth one? She began counting the trees with the splotchy bark. At number eight she stopped and read the names written on the stone. It was a licorice-black stone with peppermint-white letters:

Jonathan William Peter van Dalen

Good. She was in the right place. That was Grandpa Forever, and beneath that was the name of Grandma Forever:

Nelly Maria Elizabeth van Dalen

And at the very bottom of the stone was something else:

Now I must go
God is calling me

Maria knelt next to the grave. She tapped on the stone three times with her fist.

"Don't be afraid, Grandma, it's me, Maria, the dummy, the foolish child, the whippersnapper, the smart aleck, the sassy monkey."

She placed her ear next to the stone and listened. She sat that way for a minute, but she couldn't hear anything. A shadow stretched over the cemetery. The sun had crept behind the clouds. Maria shivered. She took the purple flower that she still held in her hand and laid it on the black gravestone.

"Look, Grandma, a weed. I picked it just for you."

Grandma didn't respond.

"Oh, all right," said Maria. "Some people call it speedwell, too."

Still not a sound. Maria pressed the palms of her hands against the stone.

"Look, Grandma, two W's. The two W's from Wake up, Wake up. Remember?"

Nothing. Maria opened her backpack and took out grandma's radio.

"Here it is, Grandma. Your radio. I bet you missed it."

She turned the knobs, but the radio didn't make a sound. She shook it back and forth, but nothing happened. In the meantime a strong wind had blown up.

Now Maria was really starting to get cold. Her knees began to shiver and so did her arms, and her teeth were chattering. She ran her trembling fingers over the tiny bumps on her arm.

"Grandma, if I stay here much longer I'll turn into a goose. Look at my arms and legs. I've got goose bumps. Pretty soon I'm going to start honking."

A streak of lightning flashed in the sky. A few second later came a peal of thunder. Maria untied the sleeves of her coat and put it on. She squatted down, hugging her legs tightly. She sat all huddled up for quite some time.

"Grandpa, maybe you're awake then?" Maria asked.

She listened intently, but Grandpa Forever wouldn't respond either. She took the plastic shovel from her backpack. If grandpa and grandma wouldn't wake up, she decided, then she'd go ahead without their permission. She began to dig next to the stone, but the earth was hard. Every time Maria stuck the plastic shovel in the ground, the handle bent way over. Very slowly, though, the hole grew bigger. Maria sighed. She put the shovel down.

The sky above had become as black as tar. Once again lightning flashed across the sky. That must be one of those false gods showing off his sparkling, razor-sharp false teeth, thought Maria. The thunder rolled and rumbled across the cemetery.

A heavy raindrop fell on Maria's nose. She kept on digging, faster and faster. When the hole was big enough, she picked up grandma's radio and put it in the ground. Then she quickly covered over the hole with dirt.

There, thought Maria, now my underground grandpa and grandma in their underground city of sleep have an underground radio with underground news, an underground orchestra, an underground minister, and the underground word of God.

Maria stood up. She wiped her hands on her pants. Her fingers were black from the mud and blue from the cold.

"I've got to get going," said Maria. She paused to take one more look at the grave. "Goodnight, and enjoy the radio, Grandma."

Just as Maria bent down to pick up her backpack, she heard a voice.

"Thank you, sassy monkey," whispered someone softly.

"Hey, Grandma," said Maria happily. "Is that you? Are you finally awake?"

The thunder rolled once again.

"Who can sleep with all that heavenly hullabaloo? I'm lying here in my grave shaking all over," said grandma. "If they keep messing around up there I'm going to file a complaint."

The lightning flashed, and for a moment the whole cemetery was full of light. Maria bent over the stone and kissed it.

"Bye, Grandma," she said. "I'll be back soon. Tell Grandpa Forever I said hello when he wakes up."

Grandma Forever had no more to say.

Must have fallen asleep again, thought Maria. Quickly she walked down the avenue with the sycamores. At the end of the path she turned around and waved to the stone. Suddenly it started raining so hard that Maria could barely see a thing. She pulled up her hood and ran out of the cemetery. It was as if the clouds in the sky were being squeezed out like a sponge by an invisible hand, Maria thought. All her clothes were soaked through. Not a single thread was dry. Maria stopped running. The water streamed down her face. She looked at her soaking-wet socks in her sandals and sat down on the edge of the sidewalk. I couldn't get any wetter than this, anyway, Maria thought. She just sat and stared.

What if I could cry as hard as it's raining right now? she wondered. Then all the streets would be flooded with my tears. And if I kept on crying, if I cried cats and dogs, for forty days and forty nights, the whole world would be destroyed by my sadness. But I'm not crying, because grandma's not dead. She's asleep. And the God of Noah isn't angry either. He's just a little bored.